A STORY FROM DOWN UNDER

WANGOOLBA

P Prince amongst dingoes

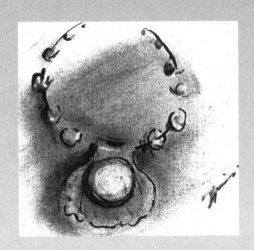

FRED WILLIAMS

ROBYN COVINGTON (ED)

JOAN GRIMES (ILLUSTRATOR)

Trafford
PUBLISHING www.trafford.com

North America & international
toll-free: 1 888 232 4444 (USA & Canada)
fax: 812 355 4082

Dedication

This story is classic Australiana material dedicated to our devoted illustrator/artist Joan Grimes who when she was just a little girl accompanied her daddy, a Forestry Pay Officer, to Central Station on Fraser Island. She loves Fraser Island and its dingoes very much and is greatly concerned for their current welfare/management and future long-term survival. She is especially concerned about the strategy of shooting them. She dreads to think about a future world without this magnificent creature.

Also, *Wangoolba A Prince Amongst Dingoes* is equally dedicated to another special person, Anne-Marie Dyer a senior librarian with the Rockhampton Municipal Library based in Central Queensland. She is qualified and a highly regarded specialist in-children's literature. She loves our *Wangoolba!*

Without both of these people's encouragement, persistence and help Wangoolba would not have become reality.

A big thank you, Joan and Anne-Marie.

INTRODUCTION

This is a fascinating and unique story about two faces of Australian culture. It is also about two beautiful islands - Fraser Island, the world's largest island of sand and Big Woody Island, a not-so-well-known island situated in the Sandy Straits of nearby sunny Queensland. Both these islands are encompassed by the environs of Hervey Bay, the whale watching capital of Queensland. It is also about two beautiful indigenous sisters and the pristine love of a Prince and Princess.

Just as places and understanding cultures quite foreign to our own are most important in this story, perhaps it is also important to point out that this story does not claim to be an indigenous dreamtime story any more than it is an indigenous legend. Perhaps it must be borne in mind that two of the creators have very long associations with Fraser Island, one having published two definitive history books on the subject, the other having published a children's book. This story is set amongst a unique and fascinating environmental background like no other on this planet – a collection of historical and indigenous culture and traditions, as well as a dominant intervening mixture of European culture within the captivating setting of the world's largest island of sand Fraser Island.

Readers will meet these two Australian characters who are indigenous sisters…

Long, long ago in the days of yore, Yendingie according to Aboriginal legend was a powerful creator of life. So much so that he created the world, its plants, all life forms and gave a special gift to the people – the magic of procreation.

Yendingie had the power to change people from one life form to another as well as possessing the power to change people's ability to live on land or in water. At that time the sisters, K'gari and Kawalo, were the appointed helpers of Yendingie. During the creation of Fraser and Big Woody, they became so taken with the islands' beauty and surrounds that they decided to ask Yendingie for permission to stay … forever.

After some discussion and a little hesitation, Yendingie agreed but said they could not stay in their current form; he would have to change them. When K'gari was transformed into a beautiful spirit form, Yendingie bestowed the new title of honour, Princess; upon her as a

AMAZING PARADISE

WANGOOLBA PRINCE AMONGST DINGOES

mark of great respect acknowledging the untiring devotion, assistance and service she had rendered to Yendingie with his creations.

Kawalo was also changed into a mythical sea creature that could only survive in the sea and Yendingie repeated the title of Princess upon her as well. Additionally, as her island was much smaller by comparison to K'gari but was surrounded by sea and creatures, Yendingie rewarded her with some additional powers that extended to power over all these creatures in the sea. Such powers were limited however, in that Princess Kawalo would not be able to leave her sea-based environment, otherwise she would instantly lose all magical powers.

The story takes us on a journey with the main character, Wangoolba (the last purebred dingo of Fraser Island), into both the indigenous sisters' new worlds and as we travel around with them; we gain a new insight into the unique experience of breathing on land and in the sea. Along the way, we meet some endearing characters such as the Moha Moha, a giant turtle who plays a central role as the medium of transport between the two connecting worlds of K'gari and Kawalo. As Wangoolba yearns for his old companion and realizes just how much he loves his ancestral home of (K'gari) Fraser Island, events are entwined with threads of both Aboriginal and European customs. What happens next brings the reality to mind of what a future world would be like without dingoes like Wangoolba.

This unusual down under story is perhaps a great example of Australian diversity that breathes education and a little more understanding into often misunderstood culture, customs and traditions, all bound by mythology, magic, history and time.

WANGOOLBA PRINCE AMONGST DINGOES

WORLD'S LARGEST ISLAND OF SAND

In the beginning several thousand years before white men discovered or colonized Australia, there lived many dingoes. From what we know, most were in the care and companionship of Aboriginal masters. This is a story that recaptures the life of just one precious individual. He was a magnificent specimen, a reddish coloured Alfa dog; his given native tribal name was *Wangoolba*. He was born and raised on a small island off the East Coast of Queensland, Australia named after K'gari an (Aboriginal Princess) that means paradise. Another of the key characters featured throughout this story is her twin sister Princess Kawalo. Perhaps, it came to pass a very long time ago somewhere in mythology, possibly as much as one million years, these twins both became islands of their own choosing during the time of the great creation. Since the advent of Europeans the island has been renamed now to Fraser Island and perhaps is a symptom of paradise almost lost certainly for our precious purebred dingo. It is a very unique island wholly made up of trillions and billions of particles of sand deposited there by the wind and sea over a very long time frame. During the time of the great creation the twin sisters voluntarily separated forever and Princess Kawalo chose to become an adjoining island *Tooliewah* (now called Big Woody) that has more of a barren rocky terrain and her special home was created for her by the great creator as a reward. So, it came to pass that Princess Kawalo inhabits a beautiful majestic palace underneath the sea with servants and all the magical trimmings. In the wisdom of the great creator, this was to make up for the small area of her chosen island that has far less unique features in comparison to K'gari.

WANGOOLBA PRINCE AMONGST DINGOES

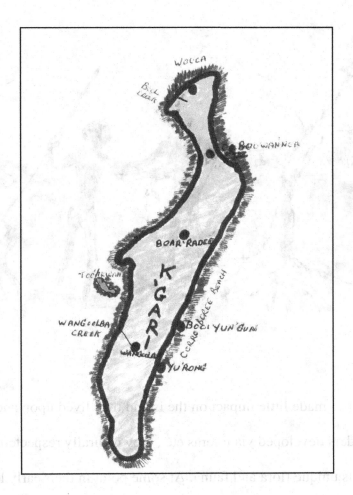

Wangoolba was blessed with a pleasant but aloof proud nature as his bushy tail often

showed, he was a strong and powerful dog. The native family that he and his pack

lived with was known as the *'Wonarie'* clan and they were *'Batjala'* people (meaning

fisher or sea folk). Surprisingly, the dingoes were also highly successful fisher dogs,

as well as good hunters and companions to the tribe. It seems in those early times

everybody lived happily together upon K'gari.

The Aboriginal tribes made little impact on the island they lived upon and nurtured. With the lifestyle the elders developed via totems etc., they naturally respected their environment and its unique flora and fauna. At some point in their early lives the elders gave them all a totem. This was usually an animal or bird sometimes plants or fish. And this totem had to be respected all their lives. They could not eat or harm it in anyway, they must protect it. When a man married he was also obligated to protect his wife's and her family totems. So, this unique system was perhaps one way of protecting the environment and preventing species from becoming threatened or endangered in anyway.

The native elder and leader of Wangoolba's tribe were called Palowarie. He was very tall and a strong leader as well as being a great fisherman – leading his tribe on many hunts to catch dugong (*Toowoora*), Palowarie was also a highly respected warrior in battle.

Wangoolba was proud to be Palowarie's best friend, mate and constant companion they went everywhere together. At night time Wangoolba slept in the bed with his master and other pack members also slept in the beds of various masters, along with their women, children and babies. On occasions if it was a very cold night, multiple animals would sleep in the tribe's beds.

Whenever they cooked fish on the open campfires, Palowarie always shared the meal like the head and guts first of all with his best friend Wangoolba as well as other tit bits etc. Some of the tribe believed Palowarie thought much more of his dog than he did of his wife, Woolamaring, but Palowarie was a good provider. But it was observed that others in the tribe also acquired the habit and shared their meal with the dogs.

WANGOOLBA PRINCE AMONGST DINGOES

DINGOES WERE NOT AGGRESSIVE

Apart from living in a flimsy house or hut that was made from bent sticks often covered with melaleuca bark for walls and a roof layered in sheet bark attached to the outside Frame, Palowarie was one of the very few to own a bark canoe *(Coonoongwa)* and that gave the family transport as well as an additional ability to obtain a regular supply of fish.

Palowarie was an excellent spear thrower – with deadly accuracy, he could spear a whiting at seven meters away.

Sugar was not known so; at times Palowarie also provided wild honey by catching a native wild bee and sticking with gum tree resin a very tiny piece of a white cockatoo feather *(Geeoong)* on its back: then he would let it go free and follow it to the hive and rob it of the sweet honey *(cubbih)*. Salt they did not need as it was readily available from the sea.

WANGOOLBA PRINCE AMONGST DINGOES

The tribe's food-supplies tendered to be of a seasonal or cyclic nature and although they had no calendars as such, the tribal leaders knew when and where to look for various foods. For example oysters were gathered when the oyster flower bloomed. Carpet snakes were fat and ready for eating when the wild passion fruit ripened etc.

Woolamaring, regardless of what anyone thought, was a good hard-working wife. She wore a dog-strap collar around her neck and whilst collecting food often attached her dilly basket to it for convenience. She worked with devotion to regularly dig yams *(woongeeang)* with a special stick hardened in the fire. Some of these yams grow as much as two meters down in the soil. She also collected water lilly roots and *eugarie* – (a shellfish) and dragged firewood back to the camp to burn.

WANGOOLBA PRINCE AMONGST DINGOES

At times when the bush tucker fruit was ripe they collected and ate it. Some of that bush tucker was *kin-man,* a small sweet white current; *no-mantel,* a kind of wild cherry; *gee-bung,* much like mistletoe and *Quandong,* a plum-like fruit. She also collected macrozamia cycad's fruit when available and pounded it and placed it in a running fresh water stream for three days to free the fruit of poisons. This was also done with pandanus nuts when they turned dark orange. They were eventually pounded into pancake size and cooked on the coals. Woolamaring was always busy preparing all the native bush tucker foods for consumption and of course keeping the camp fires burning.

 Then there were the children to attend to: three boys and two girls. Luckily, there were no clothes to wash. Bathing was conducted in the streams and sea. The children had their games and played them at any opportunity. A game like hide and seek was always popular but it was more of a tracker game that prepared them with special skills that could be used in later life. Jumping and running as well as the boys wrestled and fought in hand to hand combat throwing small spears at targets to test their strength and prepare them for the great fights. The girls collected objects and traded them with each other. As the children often accompanied their mother the games would take place as she went about the business of gathering daily food. Refrigeration was not known which is the reason food collecting or gathering was a daily activity. At meal times, the family ate with their fingers and they shared the spoils with their companion dingoes. The dingoes never became aggressive as a result of hand feeding and as mentioned earlier, often slept safely with the babies. Their life-style was simple and uncomplicated as they used readily available material as their resources. They were not ashamed of their nakedness.

header number at top

CARED FOR ORPHANED DINGOES

WANGOOLBA PRINCE AMONGST DINGOES

Sometimes if it was very cold, hot ashes from the fire would be scraped into the sand bed to warm it up. Sheets of bark were also used as blankets. Tools like grinding stones or hammers were treasured and had to be quarried elsewhere and carried to K'gari because it is a sand island without a ready supply of rock. Interestingly, you could always tell whenever Palowarie was in camp as his spears would be stuck in the sand just outside the door of his hut/home.

The men each had different responsibilities, like tool making hunting and fishing etc. Some times they walked many kilometers. If they went on another tribe's territory, permission had to be obtained.

One day, very early in the morning after camping at a neighbour's tribe for the night, Palowarie and Wangoolba set off and began walking together along *Corroboree Beach* where the tribes met annually at their great fights. Sometimes on these special occasions it would be nothing to see around four kilometers of powerful tribesmen gathered along the beach. This was a time when trading and bartering took place, some fought for a wife or just honour. This popular spot on the beach was called *(Yurong)* Eurong (that means a place of rain) and they were heading north for a big clump of rocks called (Booiyun'gun) *Poyungun Rocks* (named after a big grub found in trees).

Wangoolba was enjoying himself, running ahead sniffing the numerous scent trails left by animals and birds. When he reached the rock, he was alerted by something. He looked ahead beyond the first clump of coffee coloured rock to see something huge on the sand. He sniffed the air and his acute senses told him it was an animal.

Wangoolba rushed back to Palowarie and started to run around him to gain his attention. Palowarie knew instinctively that something was wrong and also looked ahead to the direction Wangoolba was now running. He also sniffed the air to see if he could detect something. As Palowarie passed by the first clump of rock, he saw this huge object in the beach clearing in between the rocks. As he neared, he realized it was a huge loggerhead turtle and that she had probably been laying her eggs in a nest in the sand dunes, a ritual she had followed since she matured as an adult. Palowarie had observed this since he was a little boy and his father and grandfather as well as elders had told him about turtles laying eggs in their sand dune nests. Palowarie's father had the totem of a turtle and therefore he couldn't eat it or kill it. In fact he felt obligated to assist it.

It seems the turtle on trying to navigate her way safely back to the sea slipped down the face of a sheer cut in the sea wall created by the back wash and landed on her back upside-down. She was in deep trouble. Wangoolba being a very clever dog licked her face, Palowarie wiped the tears from around her eyes and then in unison they tried to push the turtle over on its feet. They had several attempts all with the same failed result. The turtle

WANGOOLBA PRINCE AMONGST DINGOES

was just too big and heavy. Palowarie had an idea. He strode off into the surrounding scrub and located this big strong straight branch to be used as a lever. As Palowarie returned with the lever dragging along behind him, Wangoolba trotted over to him and grabbed the sticks end in his mouth to assist.

They finally positioned it under the turtle then pushed and pushed and pulled with all their joint strength until the turtle was at last flipped over on its feet. Palowarie and Wangoolba were so very pleased and Wangoolba again licked the face of the turtle before it departed instinctively in the direction of the Pacific Ocean. Palowarie felt so pleased that they had saved the turtle, considered to be an old tribal family friend, from what would have been its certain death. In line with Palowarie's tribal tradition, he found the turtle nest and removed a small number of its eggs to consume but by far the majority of the eggs were left to hatch and guarantee the survival of the species. They sat down on a small near-by sand-dune to rest for a moment or two whilst enjoying their breakfast of turtle eggs, casually gazing towards the crystal clear blue ocean as their saved friend swam farther and farther away surfacing every now and then for air. On the wind the sound of, *"Thank you, thank you,"* seemed to drift back to them, but the rescuers dismissed this as coincidence. Turtle eggs are considered a great delicacy in tribal life and to be sharing them made Wangoolba also feel very proud to be Palowarie's friend and companion.

Many, many moons passed by and on one fine spring morning, Palowarie decided he would go walkabout and see family and old friends at ' *Wocco'* (meaning a mopoke Possom), a place right on the northern tip of K'gari (Ca'ree) (Sandy Cape). It was a very long walk and it took several days. They passed by a beautiful freshwater lake called (*Boar'radee* meaning big bad hill) Bowarrady where they stayed with the hospitality of a neighbouring tribe. Here the forest was vast and some of the sandy slopes very steep and

WANGOOLBA PRINCE AMONGST DINGOES

rugged. At night time it was often cold and raining but thanks to the tribes' bark huts

warm fires and bark blankets, and of course sleeping together Wangoolba and Palowarie

were able to protect themselves from the cold night. The next day they left as the sun rose

over the vast dunes and by late in the afternoon they had reached what is now called Bool

Creek where they rested a while and quenched their thirst. After this, they had only a short

walk along the beach to reach *'Wocco'*.

The 'Wocco' tribe was very happy to see them and decided to put on a corroboree to

celebrate. The elders sent out some warriors to catch some fish and the women hurriedly

dug yams, gathered firewood, collected water lilly roots and others dug for eugarie. All

the dingoes were very excited by the visit and the activity. Wangoolba was busy smelling

all his old friends and playing catch and lick. He didn't need a wash that day to remove all

that sand from travelling as his face was licked shining clean over and over by all his old

friends and foes. At times when the games went too far for his liking, Wangoolba would

exercise his Alfa dominance and strength over all concerned. No one seemed to mind and

eventually all the dingoes joined their masters around the campfires for the evening meal.

The feasting, singing and dancing of the corroboree lasted long into the night and it wasn't

until the very early hours that the v-boom, v-boom of the possum skin drums, click sticks

and the haunting digeridoo were finally silenced. By this time all the dingoes were all

sound asleep with their masters their wives and babies. The moon was high and at last the

stars twinkled in silence the great creator seemed pleased.

Very early next morning, Wangoolba was wide-awake. Stretching and yawning, he saw

that no one was about yet so he thought he would take a walk before breakfast along the beach. Glancing at Palowarie he could see he was still exhausted from the previous night's socialising, so he went for a stroll. As he sniffed the trails at the base of the huge sand dunes around Wocca, he thought he heard a voice call out his name. But he shook his head and wiggled his pointy ears he dismissed it and thought he must be dreaming. Then as he began to enter the sandy curve of the vast golden beach, he heard it again but this time, much clearer. *"Wangoolba, Wangoolba,"* He was quite shocked by this and turned his pointy ears to the direction of the sound to discover a massive giant turtle resting on the edge of the water. In the light of the breaking morning it gleamed silvery and chocolate and as he got closer the giant Moha – Moha said, *"Wangoolba, Wangoolba, jump up on my back. Princess Kawalo wants to meet you."*

"W-who m-me? No way," said Wangoolba. *"Do you think I'm crazy? I'm not getting up there, anyway I would drown and besides I don't know any Princess Kawalo."* Wangoolba was stunned and rubbed his eyes first with his right then left paw incase he was dreaming. And then the Moha-Moha said, *" You may not know her but she knows you and wants to meet you so she can thank you in person for saving her favourite Auntie's life at Poyungun Rock recently."*

"Oh!" said Wangoolba thinking hard. *"Oh, Yes I remember now that turtle that was upside down."*

"Yes! Come on, climb aboard and I'll take you to her. I promise you won't drown as long as you're wearing this magic necklace of Princess Kawalo's. Here Wangoolba, show some faith and put it on and place your head under water and you will see what I mean."

WANGOOLBA PRINCE AMONGST DINGOES

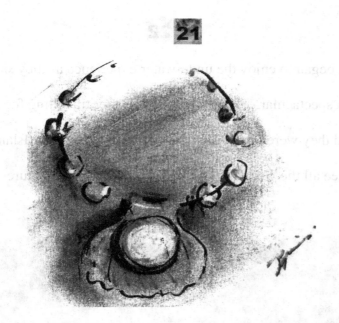

Wangoolba reluctantly took the necklace and placed it over his head, he couldn't see how it could possibly work. But to Wangoolba's great surprise and somewhat misbelief it worked and somehow he could magically breathe. After a few minutes under water Wangoolba pulled his head up and said, *"Amazing! How does it work?"*

Once again the Moha – Moha said invitingly," *Come on Wangoolba, jump up on my back."*

So a nervous Wangoolba climbed up onto the top of the giant carapace and then the Moha – Moha said, *"Hang on tight."* Wangoolba made himself as comfortable as he could right up on top of the turtle's carapace and hung on with his paws clinging to the lip of the shell. Then with a slight jerky movement, the giant turtle moved towards deeper water as the sun glistened off its scale like reflective body. *"Hold on now- here we go,"* the giant Moha-Moha said. Then with an almighty flick of its huge tail, they were propelled out and glided down under the sea effortlessly without resistance. Wangoolba was quite terrified at first but slowly began to relax as he discovered he could breathe as he had been promised with the magic of Princess Kawalo's necklace.

In fact Wangoolba began to enjoy the underwater experience as they slipped past all sorts of tropical fish and spectacular coloured seaweeds. After travelling for some time, Wangoolba figured they were approaching an area off Big Woody Island (*Tooliewah*) because he could see all the wonderful coral and a myriad sea creatures.

Suddenly, he saw an exquisite palace fully decorated and surrounded by large razor shells (*Bin-go*) while an army of soldier crabs (*Ying-ee*) guarded the entrance. The giant glided gently inside the open gates and came to a stop at a splendid sparkling golden beach. After Wangoolba released his grip and climbed down from his unusual passenger seat on the giant turtle, he was greeted by two mantis-shrimps who beckoned him to follow. Wangoolba soon discovered that the beach sparkled because of all the baby oyster shells, rich with luscious pearls as he trotted along behind the mantis-shrimps escort. Soon, they came to a huge courtyard where he was told, *"Wait here,"* for an audience with Princess Kawalo.

WANGOOLBA PRINCE AMONGST DINGOES

Wangoolba hardly had time to catch his breath when a side door opened and a syrup sweet

voice wafted to him. *"Hello Wangoolba. I'm Princess Kawalo, I'm so pleased to meet*

you."

"Oh! Princess! Likewise. Gosh!" Wangoolba exclaimed. *"You're so beautiful."*

"Well, thank you," she said politely. Wangoolba was immediately falling in love with the

Princess. Trying not to show his true feelings he asked, *"Why did you send the Moha –*

Moha to bring me here?"

"Well," said the Princess. *"Do you remember saving a big old turtle from certain death*

on the ocean beach at Booiyun'gun (Poyungun Rocks) not so long ago?"

"Yes, Yes," said Wangoolba.

The Princess continued, *"That was a very dear relation of mine and I decided to invite*

you here so we could meet face to face and I could personally thank you."

"Oh! My goodness," said Wangoolba. *"Who would ever believe this story?"*

The Princess glided over and picked up his right front paw and kissed it ever so sweetly.

Wangoolba trembled with delight and he could feel his face going a little red. *"Come,"*

she said clasping his paw in her hand gently. *"I'll show you around my underwater*

home." Well, the time just slipped by as the Princess toured Wangoolba all around the

palace and its surrounds. She even showed him her stable of racing humpback whales and

rare white whales, used by her on only special occasions. They talked and walked and

talked some more. Two giant squid bought them some tea and sea-cake as they sat on

empty turtle shells in a romantic hanging seaweed garden. Wangoolba just couldn't help

himself. He had fallen totally in love with the Princess, so he said, *"I know this sounds rather unusual, especially me being a dingo and you being a Princess and all, but I can't help it. I've fallen totally in love with you. Will you marry me?"*

The Princess looked straight into the big brown eyes of Wangoolba and then embraced him, giving him at the same time a passionate kiss. Then she whispered in his pointy ears, *"Yes Wangoolba my dear. I will marry you."* Wangoolba was so happy he almost jumped out of his skin.

Later, when this announcement was made to the staff, the palace's personal secretary took charge and appointed a time and hour and the trumpeter fish was sent forth to bugle the good news and announce it to the entire kingdom. A grand wedding ceremony and affair the likes of which the palace had never seen before since creation was infinitely planned in every detail.

On that memorable wedding day some of the guests came riding giant sharks (*Bowal*), others on giant manta rays. The transport parking area swelled with every imaginable mode of transport. The wedding carriage, a giant clamshell encrusted with sparkling pearls, was pulled by two magnificent identical twin humpback whales. The escorts were two rare white whales. The bride wore a dress of tiny baby pearls and finely woven seaweed silk-like textile designed by the finest couture in the kingdom, Sir Barra Couta. Her long flowing hair was woven and combed with layers of oyster pearls courtesy of the finest coiffure in the land, Madame Butterfly Fish. The groom wore his natural reddish suit that was brushed until it was a shining and bright. Sucker fish curled up the coat giving it an instant curl. The two attending hermit crabs fussed over the rest of his needs - they polished his nails bright black, brushed his bushy tail and fitted him with a very

WANGOOLBA PRINCE AMONGST DINGOES

WANGOOLBA PRINCE AMONGST DINGOES

special creation - a matching bow tie fashioned by Princess Kawalo's personal royal appointed jeweler. It was from an ancient sea horse encrusted with polished turtle shell and inlaid mother of pearl, a family heirloom from her Grandmother.

A feast fit for a Princess was prepared, the palace's finest chefs created exquisite cuisine from hors d'euvre, seafood cocktail, bouillabaisse, oysters a la natural, crayfish Newburg. Sweets were crepes suzettes, syabub and zabaglione. The wedding cake was a grand masterpiece creation, a three-tier cake mounted on the standing tails of twenty blue Damsel Fish with pearls in their mouths and around its perimeter, 50 Archer fish acted like guards. The centerpiece was a pair of delicate Fairy cod embracing and kissing. It was a right royal affair a declared public holiday in the kingdom and everyone was invited. The organist at the chapel was a giant squid dressed in top hat and tails an accomplished pianist who could play a unique rendition of Felix Mendelssohn's wedding march as good as any maestro. Finally, the chapel was filled with guests and others spilled onto the steps and surrounding grounds. The atmosphere was one of joy, happiness and laughter. The Reverend Tommy Cuttle of Oyster Shell Cove officiated and was also the appointed master of ceremonies. The rings (or dulings as Wangoolba knew them) were shells cut and fashioned from golden and black mother-of-pearl shell the matching pair was crafted by the kingdom's appointed royal jeweler. Wangoolba had one uniquely designed for the second toe of his left paw. When the appropriate moment came in the ceremony as the Reverend Cuttle pronounced them Dingo and wife, they were engulfed in their happiness. As Wangoolba lifted the veil of Princess Kawalo, he whispered, *"You're so beautiful,"* then kissed her very passionately while everyone attending applauded the new couple.

After the ceremony they walked down the aisle hand in paw as the crowd cheered and clapped repeatedly. At the curved ornate entrance doorway of the Chapel the Trumpeter fish announced, *"Ladies and Gentlemen may I present Prince Wangoolba and Princess Kawalo."* The Chapel bells began to chime. The crowd went wild and threw showers of sea flowers and scented petals. The electric eel and cuttle fish changed colours over and over. The surrounding coral blew bubbles and the clown fish (Yeerall) did loop to loops. A parade of colourful tiny fish darted by in large schools. It was a spectacular sight.

MARRIES THE PRINCESS

At that moment Wangoolba, the first purebred dingo in the recorded history of the entire world, was to become henceforth by marriage Prince Wangoolba.

For their honeymoon, they went on grand tour transported by a school of flying fish. They stayed at the finest "under the sea" hotels in suites like the *'Marlin Rouge'* and *'Fitzroy Garpike'* and well-known hotels *like 'Diana's Wrasse'*, *'Amberjack'*, and *'Batfish Castle'* the best the kingdom had to offer. Visiting all the wonderful Sights, at night they attended shows like *'The Convict Surgeon'* and *'Emperor King'*. For laughs they saw the comedy plays like *'Clown Fish'*, *'Dingo fish'* and *'Happy Moments'*. Musical shows like *'Fiddler'*, *'Banana Jew'* and *'Once a Jolly-tail'*. Then they proceeded onto other underwater world class attractions *like 'Jungle Perch'*, *'Madame X'* and rode the famous *'Big Lipper'*. They visited the Great Barrier Reef islands like nearby Lady Elliott and Lady Musgrave Islands, even touring as far as Great Keppel Island and the Whitsundays…

So many years of happiness slipped on by and Prince Wangoolba still deeply loved the Princess. However, something was eating away at Wangoolba. A kind of loneliness, as his mind used to drift back to all his friends on K'gari and his great companion and best friend, Palowarie. He couldn't help it and wondered if they were all right.

Concerned, one day he began talking to Princess Kawalo about the fate of his friends and she could see that Wangoolba's heart was aching more and more as he grew home sick for his friends. The Princess put her arms around him ever so tightly and looked into his big brown eyes. *"Would you like to go back and visit them Wangoolba?"* she asked.

"Oh yes please, may I do that?" he answered.

Then Princess Kawalo said, *"More years than you may realise have passed and you must prepare yourself."*

"I know," said Wangoolba. So the next day, hand in paw, they returned to that sparkling beach that he arrived on and Wangoolba saw the giant Moha – Moha waiting there. As they embraced in departure, Princess Kawalo's tears rolled onto Wangoolba's wet black nose as she whispered, *"Go my dear, God speed."* Then, she slipped over his neck her magic necklace and smiled sweetly. With that Wangoolba climbed onto the Moha – Moha's back and they slipped silently away. Wangoolba's knees were trembling and he was too frightened to wave goodbye in case he slipped off the giant turtle's carapace.

RETURNS TO K'GARI

On return to Wocco things looked far different. Wangoolba could see a giant lighthouse towering over the little bay. He could see the huge structure and two boats bobbing about and 4WDvehicles on the beach with many white people although he had no idea what in the world they were. After he climbed down from the Moha – Moha he passed Princess Kawalo's magic necklace back to the Moha Moha for safe keeping. The Moha Moha then said, *"Don't forget Wangoolba I'm here most mornings for early breakfast if you want me."*

"Alright. Thanks so much," and waved it farewell. Walking up the beach he asked himself, *"All these strangers, who are they?"* Then he called out, *"Palowarie are you there? Woomingela are you there?"* (Woomingela was Palowarie's relation). No one answered and he saw no sign or any trace of his old friends. He didn't understand it and let out a howl call to his dingo friends but they did not answer his call either. Wangoolba

WANGOOLBA PRINCE AMONGST DINGOES

was confused so he headed straight for the old Aboriginal campsite at the back of the lighthouse called *Geelg'ann* but found no one and no signs of recent camp fires, only overgrown scrub, trees and grass. In a near-by clump of Cypress Pine trees (*Coolooloi*) he spotted a carpet snake (*Wang-aan*) which was Palowarie's Aboriginal totem. Knowing that he would be trustworthy he decided to approach him and ask for assistance. Perhaps he could help in someway or maybe knew where his Wocco friends were or where the tribe had gone or where Woomingela or Palowarie were now.

The snake did not answer that very long question at first and just hissed at Wangoolba. So, he tried again and said, *"My name is Wangoolba. Do you know where my Wocco friends are or where the Aboriginal tribe has gone that used to camp here? I am looking for my friends."* When Wangoolba asked the carpet snake (*Wang-aan*) questions, he did not answer. So, he tried once more confident that he might answer, *"My name is Wangoolba. I am looking for my friends."*

"Where did you loossse them? What do they look like? Where about do they live exactly?" the snake asked.

So, Wangoolba told the snake all about Palowarie and his tribal friends. As he finished telling his story, the snake's eyes widened in disbelief and then the snake said, *"What did you sssay your name wasss?"*

"Wangoolba," he replied.

Dumbfounded, the snake stared at Wangoolba as his scales began to stand on end.

"Sssso. You're the one!"

"I'm the one what?" Wangoolba asked, confused.

WANGOOLBA PRINCE AMONGST DINGOES

"You must be the one my father told me about, just like hisss father told him. Thisss isss amazing. You were suppossssed to have dissssappeared. Your ssstory hasss become a tribal and animal legend." Now it was Wangoolba's turn to be dumbfounded but the snake continued to explain.

"When your friend, Palaworie, couldn't find you, he wasss devassstated and called for you for daysss. Legend hasss it that he did not ever ssstop looking for you. He never gave up hope of finding you and ssso, before he wasss killed, your legend wasss borne. He gave hisss children your ssstory ssso that they might continue the sssearch."

"What? 'What do you mean? I've only been away a few years."

"No my friend. It isss now the 21 Century. You disssappeared over 200 yearsss ago." Wangoolba's eyes rolled and his jaw dropped. *"No, no, no."* He lifted his head to the moon and softly howled in distress.

"You mean I'll never see Palaworie again?" he asked the snake.

"I'm afraid not," replied the snake. Then he told Wangoolba about all that had happened according to the stories that had been passed down to him. And then came the saddest news of all.

"Be brave Wangoolba for you are the lassst of a purebred line. Alasss, your friendsss and relationsss have all disssappeared. One by one, they have fallen victim to hunger and ssstarvation or the white man'sss ssspitting fire ssssticks."

The shock of it all affected Wangoolba deeply. He felt angry and was so upset by the news that he began to shake, howl and sob violently. The snake tried to console him and muffle the sound of Wangoolba's howling by coiling his body around his muzzle. All the

THIS HATED ANIMAL

while, he urged him to keep quiet because he knew the howling might attract one of those white men rangers with a fire spitting stick that made a loud noise and killed.

But it was too late. Wangoolba shook the snake off and ran off howling and sobbing. The commotion echoed into the surrounding valley and hills and it wasn't long before Wangoolba had attracted the rangers' attention and they came out with their fire sticks. B-a-n- g! B-a-n-g! As echoes rang out through the valley, Wangoolba felt agonizing, paralysing pain rushing through his body as his legs folded uncontrollably from under him. Bleeding and motionless, he realised he couldn't feel his back legs. The carpet snake, puffing terribly, finally caught up with him and slithered along side

"Wangoolba isss there anything I can do for you?" Slithering over him the snake soon found the mortal wound. *"Wangoolba, Wangoolba. You're ssstill alive, both of your back legsss are broken."* Remembering seeing how some people used splints in accidents he had witnessed he said, *"Maybe I can do the same and find sssome wood sssticks and*

WANGOOLBA PRINCE AMONGST DINGOES

sssome (Taleerba) vine and make a sssplint for them." Wangoolba did not answer so the snake slithered away. He returned after a long time with sticks and (*Taleerba*) vine trailing from his mouth, then set about quietly placing them and binding Wangoolba's legs. The snake used his coiling body to gently bind up his legs. By this time, the bleeding was almost stopped but the snake was concerned about the state of the wounds. Then the snake said to Wangoolba, *"You ressst now and ssstay quiet I'll get sssome help."* Again Wangoolba did not answer.

Many hours passed by as Wangoolba drifted in and out of consciousness. Luckily the rangers with spitting fire sticks had left. From a nearby lake the snake got six volunteers, selecting the largest and strongest long-necked turtles he could find to come and help. They planned to carry Wangoolba to the edge of (*Boowan'nor*) Ocean Lake where he would be safe temporarily.

On arrival, it was getting dark and the snake called out, *"Wangoolba, Wangoolba. I'm coming with friendsss to help you."* Wangoolba stirred as he slowly revived from shock. *"How are you Wangoolba?"* asked the snake.

Wangoolba answered softly, *"I'm still alive."*

The snake then said to Wangoolba, *"Try and lift up a bit Wangoolba, if you can, ssso thessse two turtlesss can get in under the front of your body. Then the other four turtlesss will get under your back end ssso they can carry you."* Wangoolba let out a big moan as his back end slid on top of the turtles. Then before they set off, the snake slithered on top of Wangoolba and held him tightly onto the turtles. And so this animal ambulance brigade set off on this special mercy mission. With every jerk Wangoolba let out deep moans.

WANGOOLBA PRINCE AMONGST DINGOES

WANGOOLBA'S LAST GASPS

They climbed up and down sand dunes, around scrub and forest, winding their way slowly to the shores of Ocean Lake.

Four hours later, this mercy mission arrived at its planned destination. The turtles were totally exhausted, and the snake was numb from holding on so tightly. As the party gently placed Wangoolba down onto a nice soft patch of pure white sand he let out another cry of agonising pain.

During the journey to *Boowan'ner* the snake met a pair of concerned stone –curlews (*Booiyoorung*) who said they would ask the pied cormorant to regurgitate some fish for Wangoolba and bring it to him. They were true to their word and a family of six pied cormorants arrived and regurgitated freshly caught pilchards (Towoi) for Wangoolba to eat. *"Here you are Wangoolba,"* the head cormorant said. *"Eat this and get some of your strength back."*

"Thank you," said Wangoolba. He knew he must try and eat, so he tried and managed to consume three and half pilchards. *"I'm so thirsty for (Coonggwal) water,"* said Wangoolba. Using an old empty baby turtle shell that was lying nearby, the cormorant flew down and scooped up some water from the lake then flew back to Wangoolba. *"Here you are Wangoolba."*

"Thank you," he said and clasping it with his front paws, he lapped it all up. Then Wangoolba fell into a deep sleep. The snake who was watching events closely detected through his sensitive tongue that Wangoolba had a very high fever and asked the cormorants if they could urgently go and tell all the animals to come and visit Wangoolba

and to bring him something to make him more comfortable. So they agreed and flew off into the night.

By the next morning, there was a queue about a kilometer long of animals to visit Wangoolba but he was weak, so very weak and his body invaded with fever, he was not in any fit condition to receive visitors. Wangoolba's tongue was hanging out and beads of perspiration dripped from the end. His breathing was short and shallow. The snake said, *"Can I do sssomething for you Wangoolba?"*

"Yes," said Wangoolba. *"Could you give me some more water please?"* As Wangoolba lay motionless and dying, his eyes partly opened and he saw the toe duling (ring) of Princess Kawalo now stained dark red with his dried blood. Knowing he would never see his beloved Princess Kawalo again, his eyes welled with tears of sadness as they repeatedly rolled off the end of his black nose.

Then suddenly without warning he let out a blood-curdling cry and closed his eyes as he drew his final breath. By the time the snake slithered back to Wangoolba's side he had died. *"Oh! Wangoolba, Wangoolba!"* the snake said coiling his body around him. *"We loved you ssso much. Why did you die like thisss?"* The snake gently slapped Wangoolba's face with his tail but Wangoolba was gone. *"Why did those white men rangersss do thisss to you. You were innocent. Our lassst purebred dingo,"* he lamented. By this time, all the animals who were waiting to give a gift of comfort to Wangoolba were milling around. The Reverend Tommy Cuttle, who had been granted the magic to live on the land by Princess Kawalo, was soon flown by the ospreys to the snake in order to help arrange a funeral and memorial wake for Wangoolba.

Princess Kawalo, however, could not come to the funeral because when she became a princess, she gave up the ability to live on the land. So the Reverend Cuttle volunteered to go immediately to Princess Kawalo to break the tragic news and seek her instructions. He returned later and found Wangoolba had been placed in a hollowed out log with lots of flowers and marestail fern branches were placed around it. He carried a card hand written by the Princess that simply said, *"Wangoolba I love you...till we meet again. Kawalo."* He also carried the sea horse bow tie that had been made especially for Wangoolba on his wedding day.

The Princess had tied a special thread from her wedding dress around the sea horse. The Reverend said that it was the Princess's express wish that Wangoolba was to wear his bow tie and be buried at the base of a huge fern (called macrozamia cycad).

At three o'clock, the funeral was conducted and all the animals came to pay their last respects to Wangoolba, the last purebred dingo. Even the resident fireflies from Bogimbah *(Bagin'nba)* flew up for the funeral. The long necked turtle pallbearers carried Wangoolba to his final resting-place at the base of a giant macrozamia cycad near Ocean Lake. On the way, birds like brahaminy Kite whistled, Osprey shrieked, silver gulls called, noddy terns flew in formation and pied cormorants showered his log-coffin with wild flowers.

Wangoolba was wearing his bow tie – Princess Kawalo's final gift for Wangoolba that would go with him to eternity.

The stone-curlew sang a medley of songs then Reverend Tommy Cuttle prayed for the soul of Wangoolba and asked forgiveness for his ranger murders. He said, *"Great spirit creator Yendingee please forgive them."* Picking up a handful of fine pure white sand, he continued, *"And now I ask you to take this soul of our fine dingo brother Wangoolba, ashes to ashes, dust to dust, sand to sea."* And with that, the Ospreys lowered the coffin into its grave - his final resting-place. Everyone then filed past and threw in on top of Wangoolba's coffin the gifts of comfort to help Wangoolba on his journey to eternity. The snake was the last in line and took a special moment at the graveside and sobbed saying, *"It'sss ssso hard for me to comprehend that you're dead. Goodbye my friend goodbye!"* Finally, the goannas (*Goochee*) scratched in all the sand to fill up the grave.

The wake eventually moved to the nearby Pacific Ocean water's edge. First to address the crowd of mourners was the totem carpet snake and he said, *"Although I only knew Wangoolba for a very ssshort time, I learned quite a lot, I propossse that to honour him, we ssshould rename the creek that flowsss from the traditional home of Wangoolba's father be henceforth known as Wanggoolba ssspelt with one 'g'. And to add another 'g' for the memory of hisss father."* The crowd all agreed and called, *"Wanggoolba."* The Reverend Tommy Cuttle then stood up next and recounted in some detail the highlights of Wangoolba's life with Princess Kawalo. He told the gathered mourners how extremely happy they were and how they deeply loved each other. Wangoolba would be missed as a very significant creature in creation and by all that were privileged to come in contact with him or were blessed to know him. He then proposed, *"In line with my instructions from Princess Kawalo, I hereby declare that henceforth the plant known as macrozamia cycad be known as 'Wanggoolba'. Members of the kingdom please charge your glasses and let us propose a toast to Wanggoolba."* Once more, the mourners chanted, *"Wanggoolba, Wanggoolba!"*

WANGOOLBA PRINCE AMONGST DINGOES

Just then, right at the hour of midnight, the moon brightened and the wind suddenly began

to murmur and some dried leaves rustled, flitting high into the air. Everyone was quite

startled and distracted. At this precise moment, the calm ocean erupted with a mammoth

splash as two identical twin humpback whales breached the surface of the water, spraying

foam high into the surrounding air so powerfully, it wet the frightened watching mourners.

After a moment of stunned astonishment, they began clapping but this too was interrupted

as the giant, Moha Moha broke the surface of the water with a magnificent shower of

flying fish which landed everywhere.

As the scene cleared, the entire gathering gasped in awe and amazement. Wangoolba was

sitting up on top of the giant turtle wearing his magical thread and sea horse bow tie! It

glowed in the night a warm rich golden colour. This time, he waved a paw and let out a

WANGOOLBA PRINCE AMONGST DINGOES

ANOTHER DIMENSION - ANOTHER PARADISE

howl of pleasure. The mourners cheered and clapped, some were feeling so happy and distressed they burst out crying. The fireflies lit up and danced in unison while all the birds squawked and took flight. But before the gathering could wave back, the identical twin humpback whales took a mighty dive, splashing water and foam everywhere and the giant Moha Moha with Wangoolba followed right after.

 Soon the sea was calm again as the mourners recovered from the amazing scene and rebirth of Wangoolba, the Reverend Tommy Cuttle spoke, *"Yes! Since 1991 it was a very sad era indeed for K'gari but a new era has begun for Wangoolba and Princess Kawalo as you can all bear witness to, albeit in another time – another dimension and paradise untouched by white men's cruelty and persecution of the dingo with their spitting firesticks."* Then, the Brolga's dropped in for a visit and with their lead the enthusiastic gathering began dancing to the curlew and mopoke band. They danced the night away in an emotion charged celebration of Wangoolba's life. The bandicoots and the goannas quickly followed the lead of the Brolgas on the sandy dance floor and the swamp wallaby joined the throng with his *Hip Hop*. Even the sea creatures like the dugong and dolphins joined in and danced on their tails long into the night.

In the very early hours of the morning, as all the guests that lived on the land found their respective trails home they passed by many *'Wanggoolba'* plants that glistened and dripped with golden dew, they couldn't help but be reminded how W a n g o o l b a had touched their lives forever and how he became K'gari's first **Prince amongst dingoes.**

GLOSSARY OF TERMS

Batjala............................ Means *'Sea Folk'* according to Tindale in Princess K'gari's
Fraser Island.

Bagin'nba........................A place on the east coast of the island in a report by
Archibald Meston (1905).

Bin-go........................... Razor shell in a report on Fraser Island by Archibald
Meston (1905).

Binngih.......................... Native name for Waddy Point in a report by Archibald
Meston (1905).

Boar'radee........................A big bad hill in a report by Archibald Meston (1905). See
map.

Boowan'nor......................Large Lake (Ocean Lake) on Northern end of K'gari.

Booiyun'gun..................... A tree grub (witchetty) in a report by Archibald Meston
(1905). See map.

Booiyoorung.....................Stone plover/curlew in a report by Archibald Meston
(1905).

Bowal............................Sharks in a report by Archibald Meston (1905).

Beer Beer........................Cuttle fish in a report by Archibald Meston (1905).

Ca'ree...........................Aboriginal term for Sandy Cape *see Princess K'gari's Fraser Island* (Williams Fred 2002) and in a report on Fraser Island by Archibald Meston 1905. See Map.

Coolooloi.........................Cypress Pine in a report by Archibald Meston (1905).

Coonoongwa....................A canoe in a report by Archibald Meston (1905).

Coonggwal.....................Water in a report by Archibald Meston (1905).

Cubbih..........................Wild native bee honey in a report by Archibald Meston (1905).

Duling............................See *Princess K'gari's Fraser Island* (Williams Fred 2002).

Geelg'ann.........................A mountain behind lighthouse at Sandy Cape in a report By Archibald Meston (1905).

Geeoong..........................White cockatoo in a report by Archibald Meston (1905).

Goochee.........................Goanna in a report by Archibald Meston (1905).

Madame Butterfly Fish........A fictional character based on *Guide to Fishes* (E. M. Grant).

Moha Moha.....................A giant turtle as described by school teacher Selina Lovell in 1891 in *Princess K'gari's Fraser Island* (Williams Fred 2002).

Palowarie...........................An Aboriginal character see *Princess K'gari's Fraser Island* (Williams Fred 2002).

Princess Kawalo....................A fictional character developed by the author.

Princess K'gari....................See *Princess K'gari's Fraser Island* (Williams Fred 2002).

Sir Barra Couta.......A fictional character based from *Guide to Fishes* (E. M. Grant).

Taleerba...........................A small vine in a report by Archibald Meston (1905).

Toowoora........................Dugong in a report by Archibald Meston (1905).

Tooliewah........................Big Woody Island in a report by Archibald Meston (1905). See map.

Towoi............................A Sardine like fish in a report by Archibald Meston (1905).

Wang-aan........................Carpet Snake in a report by Archibald Meston (1905).

Wanggoolba....................Macrozamia cycad see *Princess K'gari's Fraser Island Fraser Island's Definitive History* (Williams Fred 2002). In a report on Fraser Island by Archibald Meston (1905).

Wangoolba........................A fictional character developed by the author.

Wocco............................Mopoke a possum. Sandy Cape Lighthouse area according to Meston (1905).

Wonarie...........................Meaning wild dog according to Constance McDonald in *Princess K'gari's Fraser Island* (Williams Fred 2002).

Woolamaring.....................An Aboriginal character see *Princess K'gari's Fraser Island* (Williams Fred 2002).

Woongeang........................Yam in a report by Archibald Meston (1905).

Woomingela........................An Aboriginal character see *Princess K'gari's Fraser Island* (Williams Fred 2002).

Yeerall............................Small fish in a report by Archibald Meston (1905).

Ying-ee............................Soldier crab in a report by Archibald Meston (1905).

BIBILOGRAPHY

Grant E. M. 1978, *A Guide to Fishes,* Queensland Government.

Kerr Graham 1966, *Entertaining with Kerr,* A.H & A.W. Reed.

Meston Archibald 1905, Report on Fraser Island to the Queensland Legislative Assembly November 8.

Rogers Leslie, Kaplan Gisela 2003, *'Spirit of the Wild Dog'* Allen and Unwin.

Williams Fred 2002, *'Princess K'gari's Fraser Island -Fraser Island's Definite History,'* published by Fred Williams Enterprises.

Additional Reading.

Williams Fred 1982, *'Written in Sand – A History of Fraser Island.'* Jacaranda Press.

Grimes Joan (undated), *'Childhood Memories'* Kingfisher Bay Resort & Village.

(Inside Back page)

Historical notes

Since 1991 the Queensland National Parks and Wildlife Service (QPWS) of Australia have cared for all the dingoes on Fraser Island and over 105 + have been deliberately killed by rangers. During this time, the service applied a strategy of historic food deprivation and because of this some visitors have been attacked while another tragically lost his life. Prior to this the dingoes historically have always hunted the schooling fish and eaten fish/offal and food from men, women and children both black and white. History has recorded no aggressive behaviour as a result of this hand feeding practice. For the dingo this all began on Fraser Island over a very long period of time about - 4,000 years ago or may be longer.

Now it seems that under new management strategies developed by the manager that the dingoes constantly remain hungry/confused and packs totally decimated, Alfa dogs indiscriminately shot. One high protein food source, the horses (brumbies), that they had become used to eating has been removed by the service. They want to eat this red meat that is laced with minerals, vitamins and trace elements and have been exposed to it since 1885 and do not now know where their next reliable meal is coming from. The remaining native wildlife on the island has come under great pressure and is very sparse.

As a visitor to Fraser Island if you are caught feeding dingoes by a ranger they can impose a $225-00 on-the-spot-fine or greater. If the dingoes are caught eating this food they also maybe shot.

 The question is can you help save these important rare predators, ancient purebred native animals from the ranger's gun or are they doomed like the fate of our other enduring folkloric predator, the Tasmanian Tiger? The Fraser Island dingoes are, according to experts, a population of the purest bred native dogs in the entire world and the government of Queensland Australia has endorsed these significant findings but lack the initiative to support the research. No agricultural enterprises whatsoever exist on Fraser Island.

Perhaps we could declare them a national treasure, prohibit guns as was done under the earlier management of Queensland Forestry where they introduced the Queensland Fauna Conservation Act 1952. An urgent review of current legislation is required to stop the indiscriminate killing of this precious native animal on Fraser Island, permitted under the complexity of a 1992 modified Nature Conservation Act.

It is a grim prospect if we don't urgently do something to elimate these questionable management practices as the Humane Society International advocates (see on line www. hsi .org). By the year 2010 we may have none left to save.

About the author

Fred Williams was born in 1941 and educated at Mentone Grammar in Victoria. Since 1969 he has resided in Queensland Australia. At the time his parents used to live in Burrum Heads at the top of Hervey Bay where Fred based his 300 odd expeditions to Fraser Island. Many of these expeditions were free range camping trips with his family extended friends and associates. He is a keen photographer and amateur naturalist. He also holds a great respect for the native folks of Fraser Island. He now resides at Emu Park Queensland, wrote this story after having visited Fraser Island numerous times over many years. Writing is a hobby of Fred's and to his credit has produced a definitive book on the history of the island. So, it is not surprising that Fred has a lifelong fascination with Fraser Island and its native animals. A member of the Queensland Writers Association and Friends of Fraser, he also supports many other associations like the Wildlife Protection Association of Australia Inc. Apart from this book, Fred is also an author of two well-respected history books on Fraser Island and is currently developing a manuscript on the current management of the Fraser Island dingo.

*   *   *

About the book

 Like a lot of stories, novels or fairy tales Princess Kawalo is a magical spirit-like character totally created by him. Some elements of the story came about after he was told of an old Japanese story related by a Japanese exchange student who stayed at his home for six months.

 Fred loves Fraser Island and its purebred dingoes and visualized how he could develop and create a unique story blending the island and highlight the desperate plight of our dingo. The factual account of a Moha Moha sighting on 8th June 1890 by a European school teacher at Sandy Cape presented another opportunity and its entwined involvement with Aborigines using Wangoolba as the central character. They were all existing elements on Fraser Island. Thanks also to Archibald Meston the Protector of Aborigines who said a hundred years ago (in 1905) in a letter to the Under Secretary for Public Lands (first European manager on the island), *"…the place names given for the first time to save them before they would be lost forever"* This story seeks to preserve those names further and some proudly have been applied here in the context of furthering learning and cross-cultural understanding. Perhaps they were elements just begging to be bought to life again in an enjoyable and understandable way. This is Fred's first historic novel for children and adults that are young at heart.

About the Editor.

Robyn Covington is a well-respected school teacher specializing in English. She is based in Rockhampton in Central Queensland, Australia. Consulting with her sister who is also a teacher and other colleagues she developed the *'Teachers Notes'* and student exercises for this story (free from the author's website see rear cover). After visiting Fraser Island, she believes that we must save our precious purebred native dog, perhaps the last in Queensland as well as Australia and the entire world. She also believes that this story is unique and genuine Australiana and should be viewed perhaps like some of those classic Walt Disney type stories.

About the Illustrator.

Joan Grimes who lives on Coochiemudlo Island one of the beautiful islands off Cleveland Queensland, Australia moved to Fraser Island with her family in 1936. They lived at *Central Station* on the banks of *'Wangoolbba Creek'*. Joan knows the plant called *Macrozamia Cycad* very well as it grew all around the place where she lived. She also loves the dingo and as a little girl saw and fed the dogs but never had any bad experiences with them. In 2001 Joan published a book about her paintings called *'Childhood Memories'* in conjunction with *Kingfisher Bay Resort and Village*. They also used her paintings for a range of wine labels. She has had many paintings published in newspapers and magazines during her career.

From time to time she privately holds viewings around the Queens Birthday Weekend (see the author's website for further information) of her artistic collections and has sold many works of art to collectors and galleries. No one could depict these very unique Australian characters better than Joan she knew them all in her heart and imagination a very long time before bringing them to life through *'Wangoolba A Prince Amongst Dingoes.'*

Printed in the United States
By Bookmasters